This book belongs to

For my boys—
Nathan, Calloway, and Rubén

# Jon Berkeley

# Chopsticks

Random House  New York

*In a busy harbor,* on the faraway island of Hong Kong, there is a floating restaurant.

It is built on a big barge and has many stories and hundreds of windows and a roof of green tiles.

Every night, people come in sampans to eat pork and fish and prawns and rice with chopsticks, and to drink green tea from china bowls.

In this floating restaurant lives a small gray mouse called Chopsticks.

Chopsticks comes out at night, when all the people have gone home and moonbeams slant through the windows. He scurries about looking for scraps of food that the cleaners have missed.

At the entrance to the restaurant stand
two enormous pillars. They are painted
red, gold, and blue, and around each
one coils a magnificent carved dragon.

One New Year's night, as Chopsticks
washed his whiskers in the silvery light of
a full moon, one of the wooden dragons
cleared his throat and whispered
down to him, saying, "Little mouse ...
little mouse ... climb up here so I
can speak to you."

Chopsticks looked up at the whispering dragon. He took a deep breath and hopped onto the dragon's tail. Around and around the enormous pillar he climbed. Halfway up to the dragon's head he stopped. "This is close enough," he said.

The dragon sighed. "I won't eat you, little mouse," he said. "I've been here for a long, long time, and I've never moved an inch."

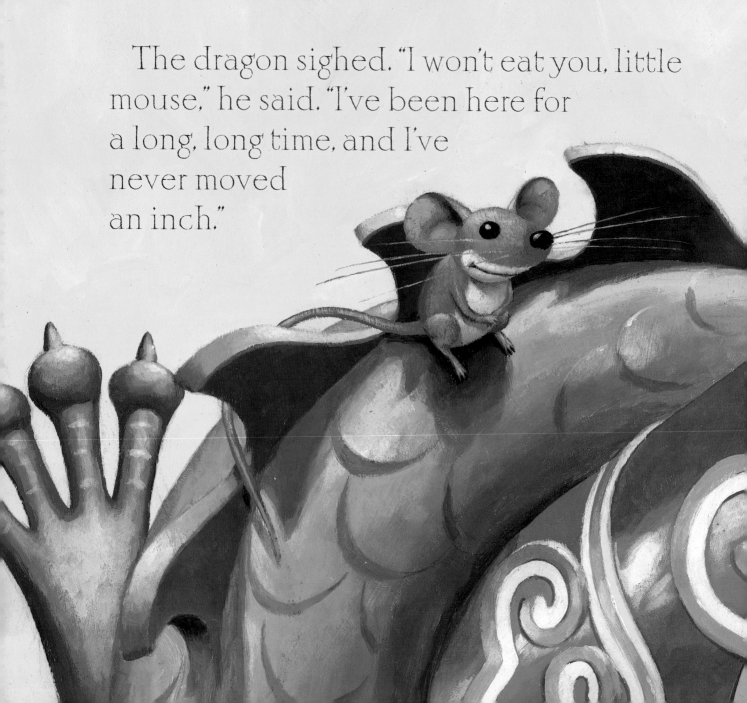

"Of course you haven't," said Chopsticks. "You are made of wood and lacquer."

"That is true," said the dragon. "But, oh, how I would love to fly. Up over the roof I would go, and over the mountains, over the shining cities and the dark forests. If you could free me, you could come with me, little mouse."

"I have always wanted to see the world," said Chopsticks. "But how could I free you from the pillar?"

"Only Old Fu knows how to give life to a wooden dragon," said the dragon. "It was Fu who carved me and my brother here, but that was many years ago, and even then he was old and almost blind."

Early the next morning, Chopsticks
hitched a ride to the woodcarvers'
workshops on the other side of
the harbor. There he found
Old Fu living by
himself on a
small sampan.

"Old Fu," he said, "I am Chopsticks the mouse, and I have heard you know how to bring a wooden dragon to life."

Old Fu chuckled. "You have come from the smiling dragon on the floating restaurant," he said. "I always knew that one would want to fly. He was the last dragon I ever made, and the finest of them all."

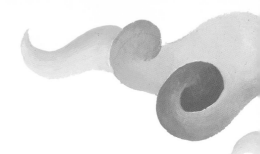

Old Fu played a short tune on a small wooden whistle. The song of a blackbird was in his tune, and the sound of the water sighing around the sampan. He played it over and over until Chopsticks had learned it by heart.

"You take this whistle and keep it safe," said Old Fu to Chopsticks. "The tune will only work when the moon is full."

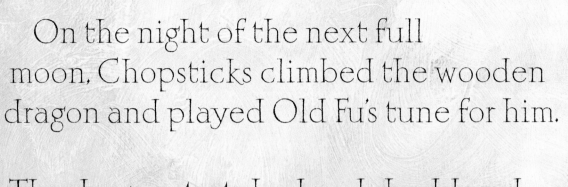

On the night of the next full
moon, Chopsticks climbed the wooden
dragon and played Old Fu's tune for him.

The dragon stretched and shuddered,
and groaned and sighed, and slowly
unwound himself from the pillar.
Chopsticks climbed onto his
nose and held on tight to
the dragon's whiskers.

Up
they
flew
into
the
night,
up toward
the smiling face
of the moon, until the
lights of the busy harbor
twinkled like tiny jewels in
the darkness below.

The whole night long, they
flew over lands that you and
I only dream of, returning to
the floating restaurant just
as the sun began to peep over
the eastern horizon.

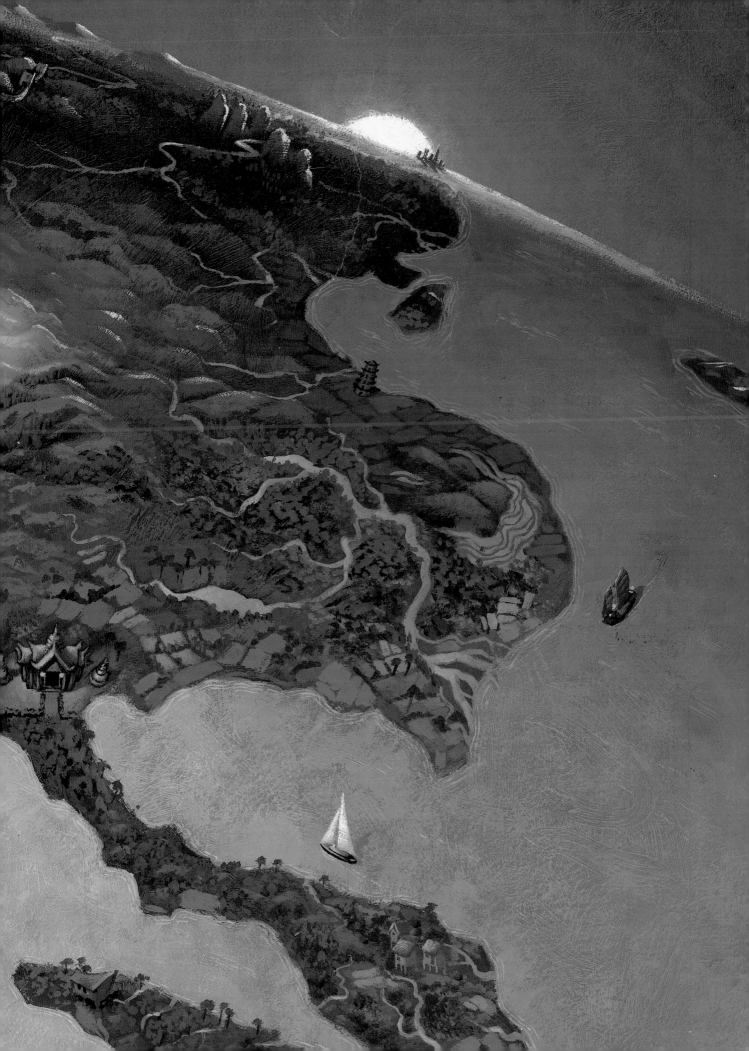

Now on every full moon, the dragon and the mouse take to the warm night air, soaring over the restaurant roof, over the mountains, over the shining cities and the dark forests.

In the daytime, Chopsticks sleeps in his favorite place, curled up safe and warm in the dragon's wooden mouth.

And after every full moon night,
he takes the story of their
adventures across the
harbor to Old Fu.

Originally published in Great Britain by Oxford University Press in 2005.

www.randomhouse.com/kids

*Library of Congress Cataloging-in-Publication Data*
Berkeley, Jon.
Chopsticks / Jon Berkeley. — 1st Random House ed.
p.  cm.
SUMMARY: A small mouse named Chopsticks who lives on a floating restaurant
in China becomes friends with a carved wooden dragon who wants to fly.
ISBN 0-375-83309-9 (trade)
[1. Mice—Fiction. 2. Dragons—Fiction. 3. Flight—Fiction.
4. Hong Kong (China)—Fiction.] I. Title.
PZ7.B45255Ch 2005   [E]—dc22   2004020994

MANUFACTURED IN CHINA   First American Edition 2006   10 9 8 7 6 5 4 3 2 1

RANDOM HOUSE and colophon are registered trademarks of Random House, Inc.